THE TREK

Ann Jonas

Julia MacRae Books   A DIVISION OF FRANKLIN WATTS

**For Susan,
and of course,
Don, Nina + Amy**

Copyright © 1985 by Ann Jonas.
All rights reserved.
First published in the United States of America 1985
by Greenwillow Books
First published in Great Britain 1986
by Julia MacRae Books
A division of Franklin Watts Ltd.,
12a Golden Square, London W1R 4BA
and Franklin Watts Australia
14 Mars Road, Lane Cove, N.S.W., 2066.
Printed in Belgium ⊠

British Library Cataloguing in Publication Data
Jonas, Ann
The trek.
I. Title
813′.54[J]   PZ7

ISBN 0-86203-244-X

My mother
doesn't walk me
to school anymore.

But she doesn't know
we live on the edge
of a jungle.

She doesn't even see
what's right outside our door!

There are creatures everywhere.
But they can't hide from me.

Some of my animals are dangerous
and it's only my amazing skill
that saves me day after day.

Look at that!
The waterhole is really
crowded today.

What will they do when this herd
goes down to drink?

Here's my helper, right on time.
Now we can cross
the desert together.

Those animals won't see us
if we stay behind the sand dunes.
Be very quiet.

That woman doesn't know
about the animals.
If she did, she'd be scared.

We missed the boat!
Now we'll have to swim
across the river.

Be careful! This jungle is full of animals.

The trading post at last!
No time to stop!

We're almost there,
only the mountain
to climb.

We made it!

SOME ANIMALS WE KNOW

MOOSE	ALLIGATOR	PORCUPINE	ALPACA	TURKEY	SPIDER
PANGOLIN	WARTHOG	ZEBRA	MONKEY	LIZARD	BONGO
CAMEL	PEACOCK	YAK	VULTURE	SEA LION	LEOPARD

MORE ANIMALS WE KNOW

OSTRICH   HIPPOPOTAMUS   KOALA   WATER BUFFALO   PIG   PYTHON

GORILLA   SWAN   RHINOCEROS   SHEEP   GIRAFFE   CASSOWARY

TURTLE   ELEPHANT   TIGER   ORANGUTAN   FISH   ORYX